PARARESCUE CORPS

BY MICHAEL P. SPRADLIN
ILLUSTRATED BY SPIROS KARKAVELAS

STONE ARCH BOOKS
a capstone imprint

DENALI STORM

A 4D BOOK

Pararescue Corps is published by
Stone Arch Books, a Capstone Imprint
1710 Roe Crest Drive
North Mankato, Minnesota 56003
www.mycapstone.com

Library of Congress Cataloging-in-Publication Data
is available on the Library of Congress website.
ISBN: 978-1-4965-5203-7 (Library Binding)
ISBN: 978-1-4965-5207-5 (eBookPDF)

Editor: Hank Musolf
Designer: Ted Williams
Production: Laura Manthe

Design Elements:

Shutterstock: John T Takai, MicroOne

Printed in Canada.
PA020

Download the Capstone app!

- Ask an adult to download the Capstone 4D app.

- Scan the cover and stars inside the book for additional content.

When you scan a spread, you'll find
fun extra stuff to go with this book!
You can also find these things
on the web at www.capstone4D.com
using the password: storm.52037

TABLE OF CONTENTS

◎ CHAPTER 1

Two Pave Hawk helicopters cleared the cover of the jagged mountain ridge. The United States Air Force Pararescuemen, nicknamed PJs, inside headed for the landing zone at top speed. Three severely injured Marines needed their help. The Pave Hawk choppers were flying on the deck — zooming along close to the ground. They traveled fast with their lights out, trying to avoid being seen.

Once the helicopters cleared the ridge, their shapes showed clearly against the night sky. The Taliban fighters saw them, and the shooting started. Enemy fire exploded all around. The Pave Hawk helicopters were supposed to have air support. Neither fighter planes nor Apache attack helicopters could help keep them safe. But support had not shown up yet. Things happened. Delays. Operational issues. Perhaps the support aircraft were engaged with the enemy further up the valley.

Captain Dave Willis piloted one of the Pave Hawks. He'd been piloting Pave Hawks for ten years. He approached everything with intensity. His dark eyes poured over the valley before them. Looking for a safe route.

"Base, this is Pedro One," said Willis. "I need an ETA on that air support. Please inform them sooner would be better than later." He squirmed in his seat, awaiting a response.

"Pedro One, this is Base," the base operator said. "Apaches are eight minutes out."

This was not the news Willis wanted to hear. Eight minutes would be an eternity in enemy territory. Bullets pinged off the side of the helicopter. Pedro One climbed in altitude. Willis knew they needed to get away from enemy fire until help showed up.

"Pedro One to Base," said Willis. "Please inform the Apaches we won't last eight minutes. We are three minutes inbound to the landing zone, taking heavy fire."

"Roger that," Base replied.

Captain Willis turned his attention to his companion Pave Hawk. Each time a team went out on a mission there were at least two Pave Hawks.

One went in to pick up the wounded. The other hovered to provide cover for the chopper on the ground. Then the first chopper would lift off with the wounded and provide cover for the second Pave Hawk to pick up more wounded, if necessary.

"Pedro Two, this is Pedro One," said Willis. "What's your status?"

Pilot Pete Miller's voice came back over the radio. "Pedro One, this is Pedro Two," said Miller. "Haven't been to a shooting gallery since the county fair as a kid. Also, did I mention I hated the shooting gallery?"

"It might have come up," Willis said.

"We won't last eight minutes," Miller said.

"That's what I told base," Willis said. "Mako, are you guys ready to go? We are one minute out, but I cannot get ground contact at the moment. Radios are probably being jammed. Can't verify if the landing zone is secure."

Mako was Chief Master Sergeant Phil "Mako" Marks. He would lead the extraction team along with his two other PJs, Airman Ahmad "Bash" Bashir and Phil Smith. "We'll fast rope in, if we have to. We've got two Cat Alphas," Mako replied.

Category Alphas—Cat Alphas for short—were the most serious type of injury. A single Cat Alpha meant trouble. Two Cat Alphas were worse. Cat Alphas were usually some type of severe wound like head trauma or spinal fracture. Patients with these injuries needed medical attention. They needed it fast.

The Golden Hour started as soon as the call sounded at their forward operating base. Once the PJs scrambled to the chopper, every second counted. The pararescuemen were 13 minutes into the Golden Hour. The patients' chances of survival improved dramatically if they could return to the base hospital within an hour. Any longer than that, the chances of more serious injury or death increased.

Mako sat back in his seat. Small arms fire pinged off the sides of the Pave Hawk. It was not a heavily-armored helicopter. For search and rescue they needed speed and agility. Armor slowed them. Extra weight might also prevent them from flying at higher altitudes. They needed to reach the injured Marines quickly.

"RPG inbound!" Willis shouted into the radio.

Mako glanced out the side door of the Pave Hawk, spotting the stream of fire from a rocket-propelled grenade headed directly at them.

"Hang on!" Willis shouted.

Time slowed down. Mako could hear his heart beat. He felt his eyes blink. The sound of blood rushing through his veins roared in his ears.

"Bank right!" Willis shouted in the radio. "Bank right! Deploying counter measures!"

Willis' voice sounded distant to Mako, like he was yelling into a tunnel.

Mako heard the pop, pop, pop sound of flares launched from the Pave Hawk. The flares were superheated. A heat-seeking missile might turn toward one of the flares instead of the chopper.

Mako, Bashir, and Smith were strapped quite securely into their seats. Their bodies, however, jerked and rocked against their restraints as the chopper banked hard to the right. Willis must have given an order to return fire because both Pave Hawk machine guns were shooting at the spot where the missile launched. The .50 caliber noise only added to the confusion.

Mako could not take his eyes off the missile screaming their way. His breath came in short gasps. Bashir and Smith closed their eyes. The missile seemed to take forever to reach them.

"I will not die like this," Mako muttered to himself. He raised his M-4 rifle, flipped it to full auto, and fired at the incoming missile. It only took seconds to empty the entire clip of thirty rounds of ammunition. Mako's shooting had no effect.

The Pave Hawk flew at such a steep angle of descent that a sudden crash seemed likely. Without warning, the chopper righted itself. The PJs lurched against the restraints again.

"We didn't explode," Mako said in disbelief.

"No, we didn't," Willis said.

Mako could hear the relief in the pilot's voice.

"Too close," Bashir said.

"Nah," Mako said. "Knew it would miss."

"Really?" Smith said. "What were you shooting at? Ducks?"

"Never mind my intended target, Airman," Mako said. "My weapon needed testing. The missile happened to provide a convenient target."

Smith and Bashir laughed.

Mako was one of the most fearless men that Smith and Bashir had ever seen. He was always cool and collected on a mission. This was their first deployment to Afghanistan.

Mako, a PJ for ten years, had been in Afghanistan four times. Sometimes it seemed like nothing rattled him.

"Heads up, Mako," Willis said. "We are at the LZ."

Down below the PJs could see a cluster of Marine vehicles. It was dark, but the occasional muzzle flashes from automatic weapons lit up the night. They were taking fire. It looked like they were surrounded.

"Put us down," Mako said.

"Negative," Willis said. "The bad guys are jamming radio frequencies. I can't tell how much opposition they're facing. Besides we don't have a secure LZ."

"We'll fast rope down," Mako said.

Sometimes the LZ was not secure for a landing. In this case, PJs would rappel from hovering choppers. It was dangerous but occasionally necessary.

"Negative, Sergeant," Willis said. "It's too hot down there."

"Lieutenant? Are you listening?" Mako said.

"I'm here, Mako," said Lieutenant Jamal Jenkins. Jenkins was Mako's Combat Rescue Officer, or CRO. He was back at the forward operating base, helping coordinate the mission.

"Loot, help us out here," Mako said. "We are 2-4,

repeat, twenty-four minutes into the Golden Hour.
We can make it."

"Negative, Mako," Jenkins said. "Captain Willis
makes the call."

Mako pounded his fist against the side of the Pave
Hawk. They needed to get to those injured Marines.
Somehow. Some way.

"Lieutenant! We have—"

Three thunderous explosions cut off Mako's words.
The noise came from the area beyond the landing
zone, from where the Marines were taking fire. The
night sky glowed orange as flames shot upward. Three
other explosions soon followed. The ground near
where the Marines were pinned down turned into
balls of yellow and blue light.

The Apache air support arrived with cannons
firing and missiles sizzling through the air. With six
missiles, they wiped out the entire Taliban resistance.

One of the Apache helicopter pilot's voices came
over the radio, saying, "I believe it's safe to land now."

"Hooyah!" the Pave Hawk crew shouted.

Without another word, Willis floated the chopper
in like a dragonfly.

When the chopper landed swiftly on the ground,

Mako checked his watch. Twenty-nine minutes into the Golden Hour.

They were going to make it.

Mako unhooked his harness. He sprinted toward the wounded men.

Six months later, a gigantic C-5 Galaxy cargo
plane dropped out of the sky. Its wheels squealed
and smoked as they struck the concrete runway. First
Lieutenant Jamal Jenkins glanced out the tiny window,
slowly exhaling.

He was a United States Air Force Pararescueman.
A PJ. One of the best-trained, most elite special
operators in the United States military.

Jenkins' team was convinced he was fearless. The
Chief Master Sergeant Phil "Mako" Marks often joked
to the unit's newcomers that Lieutenant Jenkins was a
cyborg—part man but mostly machine.

After seeing Jenkins in action, some of them
believed it. Jenkins acted like a coiled spring. He
seemed ready at any moment to parachute, swim,
hike, or helicopter in behind enemy lines. He would
climb to the top of a mountain or through a jungle

into a smoking hot desert. Jenkins would run toward enemy fire, in bad weather, during the most dangerous conditions possible, to rescue two-dozen patients by himself. The more dangerous the mission, the better. Jenkins had incredible stamina, knowledge, and was a born leader. The ways he found to keep his men motivated to remain cool under fire never ceased to amaze them. He would go anywhere, do anything at any time when it came to a rescue mission. He would do it gladly, without hesitation. He trained around the clock to always be ready. Lieutenant Jenkins lived the PJ creed: "These things we do, so that others may live."

But Jenkins had one slight flaw. He hated flying in the C-5. Flying didn't bother him. Flying in the C-5 did. To him it was just too big to get off the ground. He never understood how something the size of a small skyscraper could become airborne. When traveling to a new deployment in a C-5, he stayed glued to his seat, hands gripping the armrests, until the plane landed. With the plane on the ground, his entire body relaxed.

Mako sat next to Jenkins. He leaned forward, glancing out the window. The window was too small to see much of anything except the concrete runway rushing by.

"Loot, Chief Master Sergeant Marks reporting we are safely on the ground, sir," Mako said. "You can breathe now."

"No idea what you're referring to, Sergeant," Jenkins said. "It's a long flight, I'm just happy we're finally here." He yawned, stretching for effect.

"Uh huh. Is that why you've been holding your breath since we took off fifteen hours ago?"

"Did no such thing," Jenkins insisted. The big plane taxied to a stop.

Mako stood up. "Sure, Loot," he said.

Mako was all muscle. He stood a little less than six feet tall and was wide as a redwood tree. He looked like someone took an enormous bag of muscles and jammed them into a human skin to the point of bursting.

A typical PJ field pack weighed close to eighty pounds. Mako could carry one in each hand for three hundred yards across a tarmac never breaking a sweat. He would toss them onto a waiting chopper as if they were full of cotton balls. In addition to his tremendous strength, Mako was quick, agile like a cat, and taught the squad hand-to-hand combat. Jenkins considered Mako one the best PJs he'd ever served with.

Jenkins was proud of his men. All of them were
rising and stretching, working out the kinks of the
long flight. Like every PJ unit Combat Rescue Officer,
Jenkins believed he commanded the best team in the
entire Air Force Special Operations Command.

Each of the men grabbed his ruck, the bag
holding all their gear. They readied to exit the aircraft.
Technical Sergeant Jose Garcia was the second
ranking NCO in the unit after Mako. Garcia was the
best medic in the squad. Every team member became
a highly trained combat medic. Each PJ went through
a twenty-eight-week medical training course. Garcia
had extraordinary ability when it came to medicine.
Especially in diagnosis. If a patient on the battlefield
wasn't responding to the recommended treatment,
Garcia usually guessed the problem. He could find
the smallest wounds. He could start IVs in the most
difficult situations. He had a way with patients that
inspired confidence, always keeping them calm. This
was a helpful skill when things were at their worst.

Staff Sergeant Frank George was a giant of a man,
nearly as big as Mako. George served as the technician
of the group, capable of fixing just about anything.
Once, in Afghanistan, the team was taking heavy fire

from the Taliban. They were pinned down, trying to transport two injured Marines. George crawled to a broken .50 caliber machine gun. He repaired it with his bare hands, returning fire on the enemy. His actions gave the team time and cover to evacuate the wounded. Jenkins put him in for a medal.

The two newest members of his unit were Senior Airman Phil Smith and Senior Airman Ahmad Bashir. They were so new Jenkins hadn't gotten to know them well yet. From what he'd seen, though, they were going to be exceptional. Bashir was the best fast roper Jenkins had ever seen. He could fast rope to the ground in seconds, while the helicopter hovered above the LZ. Once on the ground, Bashir could provide covering fire until the rest of the team was safely away.

Smith looked like he was going to be good at everything. He was a strong swimmer. He jumped out of airplanes like a madman. So far, he hadn't quite bested Mako in their hand-to-hand combat drills, but he was coming a lot closer than anyone would have believed. The best shot on the team, he knew everything about weapons. In an emergency, he served as the team sniper, giving them cover against enemy forces until they completed their mission.

The thing Jenkins loved most about his squad was that every one of them was driven to be the best. They took pride in all that they did, devoting themselves to their work and the mission. Each time they went out, they were determined to bring their patients back alive.

The rear cargo hatch of the C-5 opened, the ramp lowering to the ground. Light flooded the compartment. They all squinted. At the bottom of the ramp stood a PJ in a maroon beret. The stripes on his sleeve identified him as a Chief Master Sergeant, the same rank as Mako. He saluted Lieutenant Jenkins and extended his hand.

"Chief Master Sergeant LeMaire, welcome to J-BER, sir," he said. J-BER was the nickname for Joint Base Elmendorf-Richardson used by most branches of the military.

"Thank you, Sergeant, we're happy to be here," Jenkins said.

"I can show you to your quarters, then the Colonel has requested you and your team report for a briefing," LeMaire said.

"Lead on," Jenkins said.

LeMaire stood rail thin, but even in uniform Jenkins could tell by the way he moved that he was athletic and strong. *I guess we PJs come in all shapes and sizes*, Jenkins thought.

LeMaire spun on his heel, leading them across the tarmac.

"So, what do we have to look forward to here, Sergeant?" Jenkins asked.

"Mostly high-altitude training exercises and mountain rescue," LeMaire said. "Your team just returned from Afghanistan, correct?"

"Affirmative," Jenkins said. "We did some high-altitude extractions there, combat wounds, couple of chopper crashes, but those mountains..." Jenkins' words trailed off. The mountains in Afghanistan, even at a distance, paled against the size of the ranges in Alaska. "Didn't seem as...large." Jenkins said.

LeMaire chuckled. "I guess not. It's climbing season," LeMaire said. "Occasionally, if a climber is injured, we go get them if the National Park Service can't handle the extraction. But they're very good. In fact, we often use their helicopters. Their pilots are some of the most skilled you'll ever find at flying these ranges. Especially Denali. With the winds and the cold, it's a whole different animal."

"How often is a PJ team called on?" Mako asked.

"It's hard to say," LeMaire said. "Really depends on the weather. If someone on a climbing team is injured, that changes the equation. The National Park Service doesn't have the medical training we do. Luckily, the weather looks good for the foreseeable future."

Jenkins didn't answer. Just when it seemed things were going to remain quiet is when things usually fell apart. He'd get his team ready for a high-altitude rescue. *That's my job*, he told himself. *To make them prepared for anything.*

First Lieutenant Jamal Jenkins learned to expect the unexpected. That's how you kept your men alive.

Approximately 1,300 nautical miles west of JBER, the still, cold air floating above the Bering Sea awakened. Currents unexpectedly shifted. A warm front from the South Pacific pushed further north. When it combined with the cold air of the Bering Strait, the two masses swirled together like flour and sugar in a cake mix. The warm moist air from the south merged with the freezing air hovering over the near frozen ocean in the north. Swirling winds made the waves appear slowly at first.

Quickly, the wind accelerated and waves grew higher on the ocean surface. Within minutes the swells were ten feet high, the breeze blowing over forty miles per hour. It moved east toward the Denali range, growing in strength with each mile.

CHAPTER 3

The aluminum trashcan crashed through the barracks. It rattled across the concrete floor. It collided with the metal bunks and concrete posts, coming to rest against the wall across from the entry door. Without a word, members of the squad jumped from their beds and stood at attention.

Mako filled the doorway, wearing sweats with a PJ hoodie. He smiled like a cat. "Who needs reveille when you have a good old garbage can?" he said. "PT! Outside, five minutes! Move it!" Mako pounded on the metal lockers.

Well within the five minutes of his deadline, the squad stood at attention in front of its barracks. Mako and Lieutenant Jenkins were waiting for them. They both wore mischievous grins while they stretched, preparing for a run. Even though it was early May, this was Alaska. The thermometer hadn't reached thirty degrees yet. The forecast called for a high of fifty degrees later in the day.

"Welcome to the Last Frontier, gentlemen," Lieutenant Jenkins said.

"Hooyah!" The squad replied in unison.

"I had myself a nice little chat with the Colonel after we arrived yesterday." Jenkins spoke loudly. "He told me not much would happen while we're here. It's a temporary assignment during climbing season. No disrespect to the Colonel intended, but I don't believe him. Maybe something happens, maybe not. But if it does, what will we be?"

"Ready, sir!" the squad shouted.

"That's right. We'll be ready." Jenkins was nearly shouting now. "For anything. Because we're PJs. So, we are going to start our stay here in the great state of Alaska with a little ten-mile run. Why do we do these things?"

"Hooyah! So that others may live, sir!" the squad shouted.

"Before we get started, listen up," Mako said. "Everybody get your gear on and lace up your boots. This is what you call acclimation to climate, gentlemen. If we gotta go up on the world's second tallest mountain to rescue some climber from Kansas City, we will be used to the weather!" Mako glared at all of them.

In a few seconds, the entire squad, including Lieutenant Jenkins, wore shorts and running shoes. Thick fleece sweatshirts and hoodies lay in heaps at their feet. The cold, with a slight breeze making it even colder, was nothing this squad hadn't faced before.

"Left face! Let's go!" Mako shouted.

They started their run slowly, letting their muscles stretch, warming up in the cold weather. They shouted out cadences as they ran. Slowly they picked up the pace. These men all passed the Physical Ability and Stability Test (PAST) during INDOC. They expected their training to be unusual. They expected to have unexpected obstacles placed frequently in front of them without warning. On missions, events rarely went according to plan, so it was best to let training take over. Lieutenant Jenkins drilled this message into his squad repeatedly.

Mako called out a cadence as they ran. Whenever they were on a new deployment, he always recalled his PJ training. He hadn't known much about the

PJs when he joined the Air Force. As soon as he learned what PJs did, he applied for the program. Their mission — to go places no one else would, to rescue those who others said couldn't be saved — immediately appealed to him.

Passing the first phase, which was called INDOC — short for Indoctrination — was a grueling process that lasted several weeks. They ran up and down mountains. There were twenty-mile hikes with an eighty-pound ruck on your back. His favorite was carrying telephone pole-size logs over great distances as a team exercise. Mako remembered how he kept his legs churning until he thought every muscle in his body might burst. Sleep deprivation was part of the training. They spent hours in the pool. And, of course, there was running, running, and even more running. That was just during INDOC.

Then the real training began.

Mako remembered one run in the Texas heat. The exact opposite climate of what they were doing in Alaska. In Texas they bundled up in heavy sweats and hoodies to make the run more challenging. The sweat soaked through the cloth in seconds. The heat was in the triple digits.

Mako didn't think he'd live. But he did.

As they ran, the sky lightened in the east. A ten-mile run was as easy as hanging a shirt on a hook for this squad. It was a warm-up. All of them knew Lieutenant Jenkins, and especially Mako, had much more in store for them than a simple ten-mile run. They came to expect it.

In fact, they enjoyed it.

━━━━━━

Eight hundred nautical miles to the west, the storm gained strength. The wind gusted upwards of sixty miles an hour. The waves reached heights of twenty feet.

On Denali, there were three groups of climbers. All of them were experienced, but they were spread out over the mountain. One group of four and one of three were on the Muldrow Glacier. Two experienced climbers were trying to reach the summit on the West Buttress, the most difficult ascent.

No one had informed them that a major storm was headed their way.

◎ CHAPTER 4

Lieutenant Jenkins and Sergeant Marks were
used to looking at computer screens to study weather.
A reliable weather report was vital to a successful
mission. It was one of the most important details a PJ
team needed before they departed. The big screen on
the wall in front of the room gave them pause. The
skies over Anchorage, along with most of the areas to
the northeast, were clear.

To the west however, a swirling mass of clouds,
snow, and water headed for landfall. It was certainly
different weather than Afghanistan. Snowstorms were
normal up in the higher altitudes during the winter
months. But mostly you saw wind and sandstorms.

"Looks like somebody scrambled some eggs,"
Mako said.

"Is it a hurricane? Or a typhoon or something?"
Lieutenant Jenkins asked a sergeant manning one of

the nearby stations. Her name tag said Morris and she was diligently studying the monitor.

"No sir," Sergeant Morris replied. "Not yet at least. It's a severe storm. Winds are sixty knots, waves at fifteen to twenty feet. Heavy rainfall mixed with snow. It should make landfall in another three to four hours if its current strength holds."

Lieutenant Jenkins did some mental math. A knot equaled 1.15 miles per hour. So, the winds were nearly seventy miles an hour. That meant they would be dealing with one serious storm. If it got stronger, the chances for real damage and loss of life greatly increased.

A captain walked into the control room with another group of officers.

"Gentlemen, welcome," the captain said. "I'm afraid we don't have time for everyone to meet each other right now. I'm Captain Martinez, of the JBER Operations Command. As you can see, we're tracking a vicious storm."

The captain punched buttons on a handheld remote. A close-up satellite photo of Denali appeared. Three red dots were blinking at various locations on the mountain.

"We've been watching the storm for the last twenty-four hours," Captain Martinez said. "It kicked up out of nowhere, and so far, it's maxed out with winds at 60 knots. But it could go either way. Usually storms weaken as they reach land, but the chances of that are lower over mountain ranges."

"Here's the deal," Captain Martinez said. "Right now, we've got three teams of climbers on the mountain. If this storm doesn't slow down, it will be right on top of them in another twelve hours." Captain Martinez pressed the remote. Several different photos of the storm flashed across the screen.

"How long will it take us to evacuate them?" Jenkins asked.

"There's no way to be sure." Captain Martinez said. "If the storm picks up speed we won't be able to get them down before it reaches Denali."

"Will rescue teams be sent in during the storm?" Mako asked.

Captain Martinez nodded. "The Coast Guard has already received multiple distress calls from fishing vessels," he said. "They expect more. Most boats are turning for shore but some won't outrun this storm. They're holding their helicopter assets in reserve."

The men looked at each other.

Captain Martinez continued, "They're asking us to stand by. If we need to go up to get anyone on Denali, we'll hitch a ride from the National Park Service."

Lieutenant Jenkins asked, "Sir, why wouldn't we use our own assets? Pave Hawks or Jollys?"

The Pave Hawk was a smaller helicopter that could carry a crew of six with three to five patients. They were fast and agile. A Jolly was one of the big rescue choppers. It could carry heavy cargo, troops, or large numbers of injured.

"Pave Hawks can't fly safely at that altitude," Captain Martinez said. "The Jolly is just too big. The US Air Force has the best pilots in the world, but they don't know the mountain. The National Park Service has great pilots, and they know that mountain like a dog knows pork chops."

"Understood," Jenkins said. He still wasn't completely comfortable using a non-USAF pilot or chopper.

"One more thing, Lieutenant," Captain Martinez said. "My best squads are off base for training. You're my first choice if we've gotta go get someone on Denali. Is your squad up for it?"

"May I answer, sir?" Sergeant Marks interrupted. Jenkins nodded.

"Captain Martinez. Hooyah, sir."

———

Further to the west, the storm pulled more moisture from the ocean. Its strength grew. Waves were now thirty feet high. The wind howled like a wounded cat. All along the coast fishing vessels and other small craft raced toward land. Some of them were ready to run their ships aground if necessary. No one wanted to be on open water when this storm hit. Wind speed hit seventy knots and climbed.

The storm showed no signs of slowing down.

◎ CHAPTER 5

The storm hit landfall like a hammer smashing a nail. By the time it reached the shoreline, winds gusted to one hundred miles per hour. The snow whipped sideways, making it impossible to see more than a few feet ahead. A weather emergency was declared.

Even before the storm system reached JBER, the temperature dropped thirty degrees. All non-military flights were grounded.

Inside the command room at the base, Lieutenant Jenkins and Sergeant Marks stood with Captain Martinez. They watched the weather pattern on a giant screen. A white swirling mass covered a small slice of the northwestern part of the state.

"Looks like the blob that ate Alaska," Mako joked.

"No kidding," Captain Martinez said.

"What is the latest update on the storm?" Lieutenant Jenkins asked.

"It's unusual. We sometimes get spring storms," Captain Martinez said. "A surprise blizzard here and there. Some cold temperatures. But not usually anything at this strength." He flipped the screen to another image.

"Most of them weaken when they hit landfall. But this one is still kicking," Martinez said. "Systems like this are basically inland hurricanes. The coast is being battered by waves. But the wind and snow are moving inland and not slowing down."

"What do you need from us?" Lieutenant Jenkins asked.

Captain Martinez tapped the keys on a keyboard. A satellite map of Denali appeared. "The storm is tracking to reach the Denali range in about six hours. We need to get those climbers down," he said. "The wind will be so strong, it could blow someone right off the mountain. I'd like to move your team to the base camp."

The captain brought up another map on the screen. "It's at seventy-two hundred feet, on the Southeast Fork of the Kahlitna Glacier. If we can get you there, you'll be able to assist the Park Service in reaching the climbers," he said.

"What about equipment?" Lieutenant Jenkins asked.

"We have all the high-altitude equipment you'll need," the captain said.

"Lieutenant, I don't have a problem going up to get civilians," Mako said. "But I need time for us to inspect all the equipment before we go anywhere." Sergeant Marks insisted everyone's equipment was in proper shape before every mission. Every rope, weapon, med-kit, and tool were checked, and then double-checked. Mako believed it helped keep his men alive.

"No worries, Sergeant. We'll eyeball everything on the way," Jenkins said. "Make sure Garcia checks the med kits. Include anything we might need for treatment of injuries at high altitude. Captain, just how quickly can you spin up a bird?" Lieutenant Jenkins asked.

"We'll have one ready in thirty minutes," Captain Martinez answered.

"Then what are we waiting for, sir?" Mako said. Jenkins and Mako saluted the captain, who smiled.

"I tell you, Lieutenant, you PJs are something else," the captain said.

"Yes, we are, sir," Mako said.

"Hooyah," said Lieutenant Jenkins. "We've got a chopper to catch."

———

Six thousand feet above base camp, the wind grew stronger. Two men looked to the west, seeing the gathering clouds. Jim and John Rogers, brothers from Minneapolis, warmed themselves over their small cook stove. Both were experienced climbers.

"Doesn't look good," Jim said.

"No, it doesn't," John agreed.

"What do you think? Hunker down and ride it out, or head back down?" Jim asked.

"I think we probably should head down. It's already getting colder," John said.

"Anything on the radio?" Jim asked.

"Nothing but static." John shook the radio and twisted the knob.

"That can't be good," Jim said.

"Nope," said John. He looked out at the darkening sky again.

As if to hurry their decision, their small pup tent collapsed in the wind.

"We better pack up and get moving," Jim said.

In a few minutes, they were ready.

"I think we better hurry," John said.

The wind grew stronger. Step by careful step, they descended. They bent into the wind to fight it as it tried to push them backward.

"We should go down at an angle," Jim shouted over the howling noise.

"Let's hook up," John answered. They looped a rope around their waists, tying them together. There was roughly ten feet of distance between them. Down they climbed.

The fall came without warning. Jim took the lead. His foot hit a patch of ice. He slipped, going down hard, landing on his shoulder. His momentum jerked his brother forward. They tumbled downward together, sliding alongside the hard-packed snow, rolling and scrambling over the frozen turf. They tried desperately to stop. But digging their hands into the snow and ice had no effect.

After sliding over two hundred feet, they collided with a large boulder jutting upward from the snow. Jim hit the rock first, hearing a loud snap. This was followed by a searing pain in his leg.

When his brother tumbled into the same leg, Jim screamed. He watched in horror as John's head slammed into the rock. His brother's body went limp.

"John! John!" shouted Jim.

Jim tried to sit up to reach his brother, but he was tangled in the rope. His leg bent at an odd angle. The pain was horrendous. They were slumped against the rock. Jim felt like he might pass out.

"John! John!" shouted Jim.

His brother did not answer.

Once the word was given, the squad readied their equipment and boarded a helicopter. It was a quick flight. Base camp was made up of tents with floorboards and Quonset huts. Buildings were heated by gas-powered generators. Satellite dishes pointed to the sky.

After touchdown, a National Park Service officer named Burris greeted the squad. "Welcome!" he said. "Sorry it's so hot outside. Hope you brought swimsuits."

Burris was a short man. His hair was trimmed close and small round glasses perched on his nose. He looked like a climber, thick through the arms and shoulders.

"I hope you've got some sunscreen I can borrow," Mako said over the noise of the chopper.

Burris laughed, leading them to one of the huts. Inside it looked a lot like the command room at JBER. There were computer screens and workstations manned by other Park personnel.

"You can stow all of your gear here," Burris said, pointing to an empty corner of the hut. "We'll get up to speed on the situation and discuss our next steps."

Once they dropped their rucks, Jenkins and the rest of the squad gathered in the center of the room. They studied the large monitor. It showed a satellite image of the mountain.

"As you've heard, we've got three groups of climbers on the mountain," Burris said. "The weather is worsening by the minute. We need to get them down. The question is how?"

"Can you give their location and altitude?" Jenkins asked.

"That's just it," Burris said. "We don't know for sure. All of the climbers have a transponder and satellite phones. But the transponder signals are out."

Burris punched up a new screen.

"The satellite phones aren't working either," Burris said. "Most likely because of cloud cover from the storm. We must assume the worst. Sometimes climbers will dump them to reduce weight near the summit, or…" his words trailed off.

"Or what?" Jenkins asked.

"Or they're in trouble. A fall can damage the equipment," Burris said. "Altitude sickness can cause delusions. Sick climbers will dump equipment to save weight. We've had cases where they toss their food and water. I'm betting it's the storm in this case, but I can't be sure. The map shows their last known location," Burris punched another button on the keyboard. The map zoomed in to a spot on the mountain.

Three red dots appeared on the screen. Two of them were on the glacier, and one was on the west summit of the mountain.

"How do we get them down?" Mako asked.

"That's a good question," Burris said. "All we can do is try to get a chopper as close them as possible. But in this weather? That's the pilot's call."

"What about planes or drones? Can't we send one up to look around?" Jenkins asked.

"Not in this storm. The mountain is trouble enough in good weather. A drone would be smashed to toothpicks in seconds," Burris said.

Jenkins stared at the map. He turned over possible options in his mind. This was unlike anything they faced in Afghanistan. Plus, there was the fact that Smith and Bashir were new. He had no doubt they would perform well. But this was an unusual situation for his entire team.

"If we can reach them, we bring the climbers down in a basket, one at a time. It's slow work." Burris said.

"What about snowmobiles or Sno-Cats?" Mako asked.

Burris shook his head. "The air is too thin for them to run at that altitude," he said. "And the terrain is too steep. You hit ice, a machine can end up on top of you."

"How high do you think you can get the chopper with us and our gear?" Jenkins asked.

"It would probably be two or three trips," Burris said. "Two guys and gear at a time. Maybe ten thousand feet. Twelve if we're lucky."

"What are you thinking, Loot?" Mako asked Jenkins.

"We split up. Mako, you take Garcia, Smith and Bashir. Get as close as you can to the climbers on the glacier. Sergeant George and I will retrieve the climbers on the West Summit."

Jenkins saw his men stare at each other. Then Mako spoke up. "Sir, you know that as CRO, you're supposed to stay behind and run the mission."

Jenkins smiled. "Thank you for reminding me of the rules, Mako," he said. "But we're in a pinch. We've got more than half a dozen climbers on the mountain. Some of them might be injured. I want Sergeant Garcia with you."

Mako nodded.

"Sergeant George and I will take the West Summit," said Jenkins. He looked hard at the men. "Any questions?" Jenkins said, using a tone of voice he rarely used with his men. It meant the decision was made. No further discussion was advised.

"No questions, sir," Mako barked.

"Good," said Jenkins. "Ranger Burris, let's spin up that bird." He turned to his men. "Double-check your radios. We have to climb with full equipment, at high altitude, as fast as we can, before the storm hits in force. Don't be a hero. Use your oxygen and thermal packs. That's an order. Any questions?"

Jenkins knew they had many. But no one said anything. They were going to do what they always did.

Save lives.

◎ CHAPTER 7

Mako couldn't believe a chopper could fly in these conditions. There'd been plenty of hairy flights in his career, but nothing like this. The wind roared. Gusts came without warning. What surprised him the most was the National Park Service pilot. His name was Travis Richmond. If he was nervous, it didn't show.

"Do this a lot?" Mako said over the comm channel.

"Yeah," Richmond said. "I've got about forty-five hundred hours and twenty years of flight time up here." He had thick, black shoulder-length hair. He was thin and wiry. Dark sunglasses covered his eyes.

"How high do you think we'll be able to get?" Airman Smith asked.

"I'm going to try for twelve thousand feet," said Richmond. "Flying isn't so much the problem. Hovering is the challenge. I doubt we'll be able to land. Hard to stay still when it's this windy."

Richmond pulled back on the controls as another strong gust shook the chopper. Mako looked at Smith and raised his eyes.

"Did he just say it's *windy*?" said Smith, shaking his head. The captain at J-BER was right. The National Park Service pilots were something else.

The chopper bobbed about like a cork on a rushing river. Richmond anticipated each movement. He guided the chopper with the swirling wind. As if he knew which way the wind would take them next. Mako was in awe. Smith wasn't so sure.

"Sarge," Smith said. "I think I'd rather land in a hot LZ with five hundred Taliban shooting at me than do this. That mountain looks awfully close."

The giant slope of ice and rock filled the window of the aircraft. Richmond smiled and Mako chuckled. "Don't worry, Smith," said Mako. "Garcia and Bashir made it. They're already on their way up to the climbers. If they can do it, so can we. We're eight percent tougher than they are"

Smith smiled. "Just eight percent?"

"We try to keep things fair in the Air Force, Smith," Mako said. "A higher percentage would be bad for morale."

Without warning the chopper plunged in the air, the strong wind pushing it down. Richmond pulled back on the stick, bringing the chopper back up. Richmond's expression never changed.

"Okay," Smith said. "I can happily walk the rest of the way. No need to go any higher."

Richmond chuckled in the pilot seat. "Believe me, Airman. You'll want to get as high up this hill as you can," Richmond said.

"He just said 'hill'," Smith said. The pilot's calmness tested his nerves. The lack of control annoyed him. The only time he was nervous on a mission was flying in. He wanted to be on the ground, where he could do something.

The sound of the helicopter changed.

"What's that?" Mako asked.

"Air is thinning out. We're not going to be able to go much higher," Richmond said. "I think I know a spot I can drop you off. It's sheltered from the wind. I won't be able to touch down, but you can fast rope."

"Take us there," Mako said.

They climbed more slowly. Richmond flew the chopper into a draw on the side of the mountain. It looked like someone cut a giant triangle-shaped piece of cake out of the rock and ice. It stood about three hundred yards across and did cut the wind a bit.

"We're at almost 13,000 feet. About as far as we can go," Richmond said.

"Can you land?" Mako said.

"Negative. Too risky," Richmond said. "But I think I can hover long enough for you to rappel down."

"You think?" Smith said.

"We'll take it," Mako said.

"We will?" Smith asked.

"Suit up," Mako ordered.

Richmond circled over a flat spot in the cut while Smith and Mako prepared their ropes. Mako gave him thumbs up. The craft hovered in the air. It was the worst hover Mako and Smith had seen. The wind blew them back and forth.

"Anytime now!" Richmond said.

Mako leapt through open the door. The rope trailed behind him. "Hooyah!" He screamed.

Smith grimaced. "These things we do, so others may live," he muttered to himself. Then he jumped out the door of the chopper, following his sergeant into the storm.

CHAPTER 8

Lieutenant Jenkins and Sergeant George hit the ground and headed up the mountain. They had the last known location of the two climbers. Both of the missing brothers were experienced mountaineers and had scaled Denali before.

Upon disconnecting their ropes from the chopper, they caught the full effect of the wind. The first gust felt like a punch in the face. With a fist made of ice. They wore facemasks to cut the wind, but it was still difficult to breathe.

According to the pilot, they were 2,000 feet below the last signal from the two brothers. The only problem was the 2,000 feet were almost straight up. Jenkins estimated their angle of ascent at about 70 percent. In this weather, it would be slow going.

"I thought the captain said there were twelve hours before the storm reached Denali," Sergeant George said.

They both wore Bluetooth headsets. The howling wind still made it hard to hear.

"I'm guessing that is an estimate. This might just be the front edge of the storm system," Jenkins said.

"Well I hope we're out of here before this little storm's big brother shows up," George said.

"Don't count on it," Jenkins said.

The two men turned to the task at hand. Putting their heads down, they climbed up the summit. Frames of metal spikes for ice climbing called crampons were attached to their boots. They carried a titanium walking stick and an ice axe. The wind pushed at them, trying to drive them from their feet. The ice and snow made each step dangerous.

Jenkins tried to raise the base camp on the radio. "Jenkins to base," he said.

No answer. He tried again with the same response. He said nothing to Sergeant George. The lack of communication worried him. Even if they found the climbers, how would they be able to let anyone know?

"You know, it's pretty cold up here," George said, his teeth chattering.

After thirty minutes, they had climbed 400 feet. They were PJs and in peak physical shape.

"During the pipeline, I did SERE training in the Cascade Mountains in Washington State," Jenkins said.

SERE stood for Survival, Evasion, Resistance, and Escape training.

"Trying to run and hide from a bunch of highly experienced instructors bent on catching me. Made it for almost two and a half days before they finally got me. Awfully cold in those mountains," Jenkins said.

"But not like this," Sergeant George said.

"No, not this cold. But the lesson applies," Jenkins said. "We have the advantage of equipment and training. Plus, we're the best PJ squad in the United States Air Force. So, from this moment, you and I are going to pretend this a walk on the beach. This is what we train for, right Sergeant George?"

"Hooyah, sir," George answered.

Up the summit they went. Each step was an exercise in willpower. Another hour passed and they cleared another thousand feet. One thousand feet left to reach the last known location of the climbers.

The higher they went, the colder it became. Their breath came in ragged gasps. Jenkins felt lightheaded, so he took a deep pull from his oxygen bottle. The feeling passed.

"Hit the air, Sergeant," he said.

Sergeant George did as he was told, breathing in fresh oxygen.

"I wonder how Mako is doing with the others," George said.

"He'll be fine. We're going to get hit with the worst of the storm before they are." Jenkins said. "You know Mako. He'll have a cabin built and everybody warming by the fire."

George laughed. "Wouldn't surprise me."

Jenkins stopped walking. He pulled a tablet from inside his parka. It beeped.

"What is it?" George asked.

"I . . . think it's an emergency beacon," Jenkins said.

He looked to the east. With zero visibility, he couldn't see anything. The snow blew sideways.

"It's about one thousand feet from the last known position," Jenkins said.

"Maybe they left it behind. Maybe they're already on the way down," George said.

"Maybe," Jenkins said. "But we need to check it out."

They moved east. They followed the signal.

◎ CHAPTER 9

Sergeant Mako Marks decided he and Smith would catch up with Garcia and Bashir. Where they left the chopper required them taking a risky hike right away, back to the main trail. Garcia and Bashir had about an hour head start. The pilot dropped them at almost 13,000 feet. That still left them a long way from the climbers.

It only took a few minutes for them to be huffing and puffing.

"Air sure is thin," Smith said.

"Use your oxygen," Mako said. "Remember what Loot said. Don't be a hero."

Smith took several breaths from his oxygen bottle.

"Garcia, do you read me?" Mako said into the comm. They were on the same frequency. But would the weather let the signal carry over any distance?

Mako touched his earpiece. He strained to hear any response. Only static. Then something came through.

"Mako . . . you?" Broken words sputtered through the speaker.

"Roger. Roger. Garcia. Repeat. Location. Repeat," Mako shouted over the screaming wind.

"Two thousand feet . . . GP . . . coordinates . . . sixty-three . . ."

The message broke up. The storm caused too much interference.

"Garcia," Mako said. "Come in. Garcia!"

Mako tried several times but heard no response.

"It's no use," Mako said.

"Sergeant," Smith said, taking the tablet. "I have an idea. It sounded like he said, 'GPS coordinates sixty-three something.' That must be sixty-three degrees longitude, right?"

"Yes," said Mako. He knew that Smith calculated this since protocol involved giving longitude first.

Smith manipulated the tablet. The line for 63 degrees longitude showed bright green.

"We know they're at a higher elevation," Smith said. "If we follow longitude 63, we should run into

Sarge and Bash. Or at least get close enough to make better radio contact."

Smith studied the tablet. "About three hundred meters east and we'll be on the line. Then we can go up until we meet them," Smith said.

"Good thinking, airman," said Mako. "Very good thinking. Let's go."

He stuffed the tablet back inside the pocket of his parka.

They hiked eastward. Their rucks weighed close to eighty pounds. They had heaters, med kits, and emergency shelters. Everything needed for a high-altitude rescue. But their gear was heavy and the weight pressed down on them. It made the air seem even thinner.

They arrived at the 63-degree line with very little conversation. They focused on controlling their breathing. Every fifty steps or so, Mako tried the radio. Still no answer. The wind picked up. It took real effort to keep on course.

"Let's hook up," Mako said.

They took out a harness, looping it around their waists and fastening it tight. There was ten feet of rope between them. The visibility worsened.

"Mako, are you there?" Garcia's voice came over the radio.

"Roger, Garcia. Where are you?" Mako asked.

Garcia gave them the coordinates. They were one thousand feet directly ahead.

"We're close," Mako said.

"Get closer, Mako. Fast," Garcia said. "We've got trouble."

◉ CHAPTER 10

Location: Denali, West Summit
Date: May 7th
Time: 1930 hours

Lieutenant Jenkins and Sergeant George had been on the mountain for close to two hours. The storm was the enemy. No matter how hard they pushed, the beacon remained far away. If the climbers activated the emergency signal, they were probably injured or in danger.

"Tough sledding, Loot," Sergeant George said.

"Not nearly tough enough to stop us, Sergeant," Lieutenant Jenkins said.

"Hooyah," Sergeant George's response was barely a whisper.

"Hold up," Lieutenant Jenkins said.

Jenkins studied Sergeant George.

"Take some oxygen," Jenkins said.

The sergeant put the mask over his nose and mouth. He breathed in deeply.

"Better?" Jenkins asked.

"Better," George said.

"We've got to keep going," Jenkins said.

"Roger that Loot. I'm ready." George put the oxygen bottle in his pocket.

Jenkins hooked the harness around George. Jenkins took the lead. He could feel Sergeant George struggling. Then he seemed to get a second wind. They walked side by side. The terrain steepened. Soon their legs burned from the stress.

A few steps later they stopped for water. They carried camelback packs beneath layers of thermal clothing. It kept the water from freezing. Jenkins felt a headache coming on. The water would help.

"How much further?" Sergeant George asked.

"We should be right on top of them," Jenkins said, looking at the tablet. "If they're still with the beacon, that is."

"Hello!" Sergeant George shouted. "John and Jim Rogers! Are you there?"

The wind roared so loudly that they would be unlikely to hear any response.

Jenkins blew into a whistle with three sharp blasts. Then again. And again.

Nothing.

"Let's keep going," Jenkins said.

Before they took a step, George's head snapped up.

"Loot, did you hear that?" George asked.

"Hear what?" Jenkins said.

"Wait." George held up his hand, leaning his head toward the summit.

The wind howled. Ice crystals pelted their parkas.

"I don't hear anything," Jenkins said.

"Try the whistle again," George said.

Jenkins blasted the whistle.

They could hear something faintly over the roar of the wind.

"Help . . . Help . . ."

The sound trailed off in the howling gale. They took fifty steps north and blew the whistle. There was no response.

They took fifty steps east and whistled again.

"Help!" The voice was closer this time.

"Where are you?" Jenkins shouted.

"Here!" a voice cried out of the howling storm. "Over here!"

The snow was thick and the wind was loud. As it turned out, the two injured men were only twenty feet away, but completely hidden by blowing snow.

One appeared to be unconscious. The other looked badly injured. Lieutenant Jenkins and Sergeant George rushed to their side and dropped to the ground next to them. Their adrenaline kicked in. Their burning muscles and headaches were forgotten.

One man's leg twisted at a sick angle, bent nearly backward behind him. The other slumped against a boulder.

"It's okay," Lieutenant Jenkins said to the man with the broken leg. "We're going to take care of you."

⊚ CHAPTER 11

Location: Denali, Kahlitna Glacier
Date: May 7th
Time: 2100 hours

The climb was still steep. With each step Mako and Smith improved their radio communication with their teammates. It took them another hour, as the storm tried to blow them back down the mountain. Finally, they spotted shadowy shapes ahead in the snow. It was Bashir and Garcia. They found the first group of four climbers.

Mako surveyed the scene. Two of the climbers lay on the ground. Bashir knelt next to one holding an IV bag. The other two were huddled together. They were wrapped in a survival blanket.

"What have we got, Garcia?" Mako asked.

"Two patients with hypothermia and early signs of frostbite," said Garcia. "One of them is probably going to lose a couple of toes. I've given them heated IV's to raise their core temperatures. The others are just fatigued with a little altitude sickness. If we can get them down, they'll be okay."

"Any sign of the other three?" Mako asked.

"Negative," Bashir said. "They're higher up. There's no beacon and I still can't raise them on the radio."

Mako looked at the group. Options spun in his mind. Decisions needed to be made quickly. Lives depended on it.

"Can those two walk?" Mako asked Garcia. The two climbers in the blanket looked up.

"I think so. It'll be slow going, but we can at least start to climb down," Garcia said.

"Okay, here's what we're going to do. We've got collapsible rescue baskets," Mako said. "You and Bashir will each take the lead. One of the climbers will carry the back end. Start climbing down. About two thousand feet down there's a cut in the glacier that will give you shelter from the wind."

"Yeah, that's where that pilot dropped us off. I've never seen anything like it," Garcia said.

"That's the spot," Mako said. "Head there. You'll have some relief from the storm and it should be a few degrees warmer, thirty below instead of fifty. If they can't get you with the chopper, put up the emergency shelters. Use your heaters and oxygen and try to ride it out."

"What are you going to do?" Garcia asked.

"Smith and I will go up, and try to find the other three. We can help lead them back down," Mako said.

"Sergeant, I think that's a mistake," Garcia said. "I think you and Smith should lead this group down, and let Bashir and I—"

Mako cut him off.

"Decision is made, Sergeant," Mako said. "We know this group needs medical attention. The other group might as well. If you make it to the cut, treat them. You're the best medic that we have at our disposal. Let's not waste time, okay?" Mako had to shout over the strengthening wind.

Garcia was not pleased. "Okay," he said, "but for the record—"

"Yeah," Mako interrupted. "I know, I know. Let's get you going."

The four PJs jumped to the task. Portable litters were pulled from their rucks. They were lightweight rescue baskets with a strong enough frame to carry an injured patient. They were made from high-strength aluminum. In a few minutes the two men were secure on the litters. Both were unconscious. Mako looked at the two other climbers.

"I'm sorry. I haven't had time for introductions," Mako said. "You've already met Garcia and Bashir, I'm Sergeant Marks and this is Senior Airman Smith."

The two men held out their hands. "Bob McCracken and Tim Oliver," they said.

"Okay, Bob, Tim, Sergeant Garcia, and Senior Airman Bashir are going to need your help. Do you think you can do that?" Mako asked.

The two men glanced at each other, and nodded.

"Good," Mako said. "You're going to help carry your friends down to shelter. I need you to listen to Sergeant Garcia. Can you do that?"

The men—ragged and exhausted—nodded again.

"Great. That's great. You're in good hands," Mako said. "Sergeant Garcia is one of the best men in the entire Air Force. If you listen to him, he'll take care of you."

The four men picked up the litters. Bob and Tim, worn out from the climb, groaned with the effort.

"Be careful," Mako said. "Make sure to stop and rest. Hydrate. Use your oxygen. If you can't make it all the way to the cut, find a spot to dig in. Keep checking your radio."

Mako tried to project confidence.

"Anything else?" Garcia joked.

"I think that covers it," Mako said.

"Roger that," Garcia said.

The four men started down the glacier. In less than a minute they were invisible in the blowing snow.

"What are we going to do, Sarge?" Smith asked. Mako couldn't blame him for sounding anxious. It was a completely new experience for him.

Mako looked at his tablet. He took a compass bearing. The last known coordinates of the other climbing team were a lot higher than he liked.

"I tell you what we're going to do, Smith," Mako said. "We're going to walk on the beach. Like I told you." He stuck his walking stick into the ground and headed up the trail.

"Just imagine," said Mako, "that we're going to rescue some swimmers."

Smith rolled his eyes and looked out at the mountain of ice and snow. "Some beach," he muttered. Once again, he followed his sergeant into the storm.

The situation was worse than Lieutenant Jenkins could have imagined. He and George immediately went to work on the injured brothers. Neither one could walk. One had a badly broken leg and bruises, and both suffered from exposure. The man passed out when George straightened his leg. They placed an inflatable splint on the leg to keep it from moving.

Jenkins checked the first man's blood pressure. George gave him an injection of medicine for the pain. He was stable. The problem was his complete immobility. They had two men who couldn't walk. Getting them down would be a challenge.

Jenkins examined the second man. Turning him gently, he unzipped his parka and checked his body for other wounds or broken bones. He carefully felt the ribs. Broken ribs could cause internal bleeding. He found nothing else alarming.

He turned his attention to the head. If his skull were fractured, he could die. Jenkins cleaned the blood away from the wound, finding a small depression in the bony skull. Definitely a fracture.

Jenkins started an IV, which put fluids into the man's veins. Fluids were essential to keep his blood pressure up. He applied a special clotting bandage to his head to control the bleeding. He wasn't sure how much blood the man had lost. Fearing a spine injury, he also applied a neck collar. He was grateful the PJs at JBER and the Park Service knew what type of medical equipment might be needed for this mission.

"What are we going to do, Loot?" Sergeant George asked him. "These guys certainly can't walk. And we can't carry them."

"I'm thinking," Jenkins said.

"Sir, no disrespect, but we better think fast. The storm is getting worse," George said.

"Roger that, Sergeant," Jenkins said.

Jenkins tried the radio. Nothing but static. The satellite phone signal couldn't cut through the cloud cover. They were alone and stuck. Somehow, they needed to get to a lower altitude. The further down they went, the higher their chances of survival.

But Jenkins held no illusions. There would be no helicopter rescue in the immediate future, even if they could get lower. The storm was too intense. They would need to hunker down in an emergency shelter to ride out the storm. He and George could not carry two severely injured men all the way down one of the world's tallest mountains.

Jenkins felt that familiar tingle along his spine. Their lives depended on the decisions he would make. Since he'd made Lieutenant, he usually directed his men from a command post. There he had the benefit of communications, computers, satellite or drone imagery. There was none of that now. He could only rely on training and instinct.

Sergeant George watched the patients. The brother with the broken leg passed out before he told them if he was John or Jim. He groaned in pain.

"I'm giving him another dose of the painkiller," Sergeant George said.

He expertly drew the medicine into the syringe. He inserted the painkiller into the IV. It would spread through the bloodstream more quickly. It was important to keep the patient as comfortable as possible. The thought made George chuckle, especially since their current location was quite possibly the most uncomfortable place on the planet.

Jenkins could tell Sergeant George was getting restless. They needed to get these men down fast.

"This isn't going to be easy, Sarge, but I don't see another way," Jenkins said. "We're going to tie our litters together. We're going to have to carry them both,"

"Roger that," Sergeant George said.

They each pulled their litters out of their rucks. In a few minutes, they were securely tied together.

"Now, let's see what we can do about about lightening the load," Jenkins said.

They removed each man's pack. A quick search revealed some additional oxygen and water. They removed anything that would reduce weight.

"We're carrying them plus our own packs," Jenkins said. "We're going to try and get as low as we can. Then we'll put up the shelters and try to ride this out."

Jenkins looked to the west. Whenever the snow let up for even a moment, all he could see were dark clouds. Thick and heavy with moisture, moving straight toward them. He didn't like his plan much.

He didn't like it at all.

◎ CHAPTER 13

Location: Denali, Kahlitna Glacier
Date: May 7th
Time: 2215 hours

One thing Mako learned in his years as a PJ: Things sometimes go wrong with no warning. Sometimes, there is no time to prepare. Sometimes, there is no hint that something bad is about to happen.

But when things went wrong, Mako knew what to do. At times like that, he fell back on his training and made adjustments. Those who adjusted, prevailed. Those who didn't, failed. Mako hated failing.

Mako and Smith were tethered and hiking upward toward the other group of climbers. Without warning, the ground gave way beneath Mako's feet. For about two seconds he heard the crack of ice. The snow made a crunching noise.

Mako was falling before he could react.

He had stepped into a large hole in the ground hidden by a top layer of ice or snow, a crevasse. The thin layer could not support much weight. Smith fell too.

The young airman was jerked by the harness, right into the crevasse with his sergeant. Neither man had enough time to properly react.

Luckily, it was a larger crack in the surface ice. Climbers who fell into a crevasse were often lost forever. They would land at the bottom or become wedged in the ice, unable to free themselves.

The tumble wasn't pretty. Mako and Smith collided with ice, boulders, and each other. About fifteen meters down, they came to a jarring halt. Smith's knee landed right in Mako's gut, driving the air from Mako's lungs. Both of them lay stunned and unmoving.

"What just happened?" Smith finally groaned.

It took Mako a moment to recover. "We fell," he finally said.

"Sarge," said Smith. "You certainly have a gift for understatement."

"Are you injured?" Mako asked.

Smith flexed his shoulder. "Yes," he said.

"Where?" Mako was trying to wiggle his way out from under the airman. "What area?"

"Is my entire body an area?" Smith said.

"Seriously, Airman. Are you hurt?" Mako asked.

"My right elbow is a little banged up," Smith said. "And really, Sarge. If I'm being truthful, I'm a little achy all over. I didn't expect to fall a hundred feet."

"We didn't fall a hundred feet," Mako said.

"That makes it better," Smith said. With great effort, he sat up and managed to scoot the rest of the way off Mako.

"Sarge," Smith said. "Are you hurt?"

"No. The hard ice floor cushioned my fall," Mako said. "Besides, I'm indestructible."

"C'mon Sarge. We need to check each other for injuries. What have you got?" Smith said.

Smith wouldn't back down from Mako on this. Smith always assessed the patient in the field, treating the obvious injury first. Then he checked the entire body for any sign of another wound. It was called a blood sweep. Even if that other patient was his Chief Master Sergeant.

"I expect there's a big goose egg on the back of my head," Mako said. "Mostly bruises. I don't feel like I broke anything."

"That's good," Smith said. He tried straightening his right arm and winced.

"What's up with your arm?" Mako asked.

Smith felt along his arm.

"It's hard to tell with the thick clothing and the parka, but it doesn't feel broken. And I'm not taking anything off in this weather. Maybe my elbow is dislocated. My voice goes higher when I try to move it," Smith said.

Mako removed an arm sling from the med kit. He carefully put Smith's arm in the sling, adjusting it until it fit snug against his chest. He tried to reach Sergeant Garcia on the radio.

"We're probably not going to get a signal down here," Mako said.

"At least we're out of the wind," Smith said.

The bottom of the crevasse measured about four feet wide and ten feet long. There was just enough room for them to stand up. Mako felt his frustration rising. Further up the mountain could be some injured climbers. His job required getting to them.

Mako had now made a huge mistake and gotten one of his men injured. He took several calming breaths. He couldn't get himself worked up. He needed to think. He had to find a way out of here.

The crevasse narrowed toward the top. Mako tried to think of some way he could climb out.

He knew that once he was out, he would have to pull Smith up. With an injured arm, Smith wouldn't be able to help much. Mako knew he had no time to waste. He needed to find those climbers.

Mako looked at his walking stick. It was still attached to his wrist by the strap. Luckily, neither he nor Smith landed on the axe when they fell. The walking stick was made of thick carbon fiber. It was light but strong.

This gave Mako an idea. He shrugged off his ruck and removed a fifty-foot length of rope from it.

"What are you doing, Sarge?" Smith asked.

"I'm going to shimmy up to the top. Then I'm going to pull you and our equipment up," Mako said.

"Are you sure that's a good idea?" Smith asked.

"It's about all we got," Mako said. "We can't stay here. If it keeps snowing we'll be buried alive." Mako said as he studied the walls of the ice cave above him.

Mako wedged the walking stick into the crevasse walls above his head. He grabbed it with both hands, like he was about to do a chin up. He dug one foot into the wall. The crampons attached to his boots dug into the ice. Hoisting himself up, he dug his other foot into the opposite wall.

Working the walking stick loose, he wedged it higher and repeated the steps.

"Please don't fall on me," Smith said.

"I'm counting on you to catch me," Mako said.

Slowly, a few feet at a time, Mako made his way up. The walking stick bent from the strain. He worried it might snap.

It took him almost an hour to reach the top. With one last effort, he pulled himself high enough to see out of the hole. He swung his ice axe and felt it dig deep into the surface. He used it to pull himself over the side and onto the ground. He was out of breath and light headed. The gale force wind hit him like a freight train. Sweat froze on his body.

"It's cold up here," Mako said.

"Really? I thought you said we're at the beach!" Smith said.

"Smart alecks get extra PT," Mako said.

Climbing to his knees he unfurled the rope and lowered it to Smith.

"Tie it to our rucks and I'll pull those up first," Mako said.

"Can you pull them both up at once?" Smith said.

"Of course," Mako said. "Now quit wasting time."

Mako waited for Smith to tie the rucks to the rope. They needed to get moving. The longer they stayed still, the colder they'd grow.

"Sometime today, if you don't mind," Mako said.

"I only got one arm, Sarge," Smith said.

"Are you making excuses?" Mako asked.

"No, Sergeant," said Smith in a tired voice. "Go ahead and pull away."

Mako looped the rope across his shoulders and fastened it to a clip on his belt. He bent his body away from the wind. Pulling 160 pounds of equipment out of a 15-meter hole in a blizzard was very difficult. Even for a big man like Sergeant Phil Marks.

Mako's boots dug into the icy ground and he strained. The altitude and thin air made him gasp. Smith was big. How would he raise him up? It didn't matter. He would do whatever it took. He dragged the packs out of the hole. Untying the rope, he tossed it down to Smith.

"You know the drill, Airman," Mako said.

"Ready!" Smith said.

Mako bent at the waist and drove forward with his legs. The wind and the odd angle from the weight almost blew him off his feet. He growled, digging in and driving harder. Smith used his legs as much as he could to help, but it was still like pulling dead weight.

Mako slipped on the ice and fell backward. Smith yelped and dropped a few feet inside the crevasse. Mako slid across the ground, trying to find any way to stop himself from being pulled back inside. He felt the handle of his ice axe. With a roar he swung it hard, driving it into the ice. It jerked him to a halt, but he thought it might tear his shoulder from its socket.

Smith managed to recover. He dug his feet into the walls of the icy shaft. Mako groaned and rolled to his hands and knees. Slowly he stood. He bent at the waist and drove forward. Forward. Forward.

Finally, Smith reached the top and with his good arm, swung his ice axe into the ground. It gave Mako enough time to reach him, and pull the airman over the side.

Mako collapsed on the ground, breathing heavily. Smith dug into his ruck and handed Mako an oxygen bottle. The air helped clear his head. He climbed to his feet.

"Can you walk?" Mako asked.

"Yeah," Smith said. "Just can't fly."

"I'll carry your ruck," Mako said.

"No, Sergeant. You'll wear out at this altitude. I can carry my ruck. Just help me get it on," Smith said.

Mako didn't protest. Smith realized that despite his injury they must continue. To finish the mission, quitting was not an option. Mako helped Smith adjust the ruck on his back.

The storm worsened.

The wind and snow tried to pound them into the ground. With everything back in place, they readied themselves to continue their hike.

"Did you hear that?" Smith asked.

"Hear what?" Mako said.

Smith stopped, tilted his head and strained to listen more closely. Over the sound of the screaming wind came the faint sound of a whistle.

"That," Smith said.

Both men listened. They heard the sound again, and then voices that shouted, "Over here! Over here!"

Smith and Mako looked and listened.

The whistle sounded again, closer to them this time. The shouting grew in volume. A few minutes later, three shapes appeared like ghosts out of the wall of blowing snow.

It was the three climbers.

Their clothes were covered in ice. Two of the climbers were holding up a third climber, who limped slowly along.

Mako and Smith rushed to them, and when they reached them, the climbers finally stopped trudging. All of them bent at the waist, putting their hands on their knees, gasping for breath.

One of them looked up and gave a little salute. "Boy, are we glad to see you," he said.

◉ CHAPTER 14

Location: Denali, West Summit
Date: May 7th
Time: 2340 hours

The storm hit the parescuemen with all its fury. The wind was unrelenting. The snow turned to tiny daggers of flying ice. Worst of all, it slowed progress down the mountain.

Carrying the two men on the litter was exhausting. Jenkins and George stopped to rest frequently. Their arms burned. Even oxygen wasn't helping.

Jenkins tried calling someone on the radio every fifteen minutes. Each attempt brought no response. They weren't going to make it unless Jenkins found a solution soon.

But what?

Fatigue and lack of oxygen made thinking clearly difficult. They descended blindly. Jenkins knew the lower they went, the warmer the temperature. He realized there wasn't much difference between dying at thirty below zero or fifty below zero.

Jenkins' body begged him to stop. To surrender. His brain refused to quit. He could hear Sergeant George's labored breath behind him. After a while, Jenkins knew only that they were headed down. He couldn't tell if they were taking a direct route. It was nearly impossible to see. They would stop every twenty yards, lower the litter to the ground, and wipe the snow and ice from their goggles.

"What are we going to do, Loot?" Sergeant George said.

"Keep going," Jenkins said.

"Yes, sir," George said.

Picking up the litter, they staggered a few more yards down the mountain. It took no time at all for their goggles to be covered over again. As they set down the litter, Jenkins lost his footing.

Jenkins hit the ground hard. The slope was steep. They'd walked onto an icy patch. Jenkins tumbled away from Sergeant George and the climbers.

"Loot!" George said.

George's instinct said to go after his leader. But training and regulations told George to never abandon the patient. With the visibility so poor, he might not find them again.

Jenkins tried desperately to slow his fall. His gloved hands clawed at the ground. His fingers were numb and practically useless. Digging his feet into the ground had no effect. He finally collided with a small boulder, jamming his foot against it. Pain shot up his leg and he cried out.

Jenkins lay on the ground, breathing hard. *Get up Jenkins*, he said to himself. *Haul your lazy bones to your feet, Lieutenant. On the double. Move. That's an order.* He used every psychological trick he could think of, willing himself to stand.

"Sergeant, you there?" Jenkins said over the radio.

"Loot! Wahoo! Are you all right?" Smith said.

"Yes. I banged my leg up a bit, but I'm okay," Jenkins said.

"What do we do now?" Smith asked.

"I'll come back. Just give me a minute to gather myself," Jenkins said as he sat up.

Jenkins looked around. There wasn't much to see but white. Except for the small boulder he'd collided with. Which leaned against a bigger boulder. Which was part of a rock formation of even larger boulders.

He had an idea. Slowly he circled the rocks. On the opposite side, he found the stones laid out in a semi-circle. They blocked the wind. It would be a good place to put the shelters up and ride out the storm. He marked the GPS coordinates on his tablet.

The only problem involved getting back to George and the climbers. He wasn't sure he could even find them in the blinding snow. Or if he'd be able to climb with his leg throbbing like a bass guitar.

"Sarge. Use your whistle," Jenkins said into the radio.

He strained to hear. Its sound carried over the wind just barely.

"Again," Jenkins said.

Jenkins climbed toward the sound.

"Again!" Jenkins shouted.

The whistle was slightly louder.

Jenkins' leg burned. "Gotta keep going," he muttered to himself. "These things we do, so others may live." Jenkins grimaced as he recited the PJ motto. Another step. Then another.

These things we do, so others may live.

The whistle sounded a little closer. Over and over he said the words and climbed. Sergeant George kept blasting the whistle.

Jenkins didn't think he could go on.

These things we do, so others may live.

Jenkins could barely get the words out. He stumbled. The whistle was suddenly very loud.

"George!" Jenkins shouted.

"Here Loot! Right here!" Smith answered back.

Four more steps and there they were. Dark outlines in the billowing curtain of white snow. He'd made it.

"Sir, am I glad to see you," George said.

"Likewise," Jenkins said. "Likewise."

"Sir, we can't stay here," George said.

"Don't worry. I fell into something," Jenkins said.

Sergeant George looked confused.

"No time to explain," Jenkins said. "I found a spot where we can hunker down." Jenkins struggled to his feet. With a groan, he lifted his end of the litter.

Down the mountain they went. It took another hour, but they finally reached the rock formation.

Jenkins led them to the natural enclosure in the rocks. He was just about finished.

"I got this, Loot," Sergeant George said.

Finding the spot seemed to energize the sergeant. He pulled the emergency shelters out of the rucks. Each was big enough for two people. It was slow work in the bulky clothes and gloves.

Soon the shelters were erected. Together, Jenkins and George put each patient in one unit.

"I'll take the head wound, you take the broken leg," George said.

Jenkins could only nod.

The emergency heaters warmed the inside of the shelters. Being out of the wind was a huge advantage. Sergeant George checked each patient's vital signs.

"Things look good, Loot," Sergeant George said.

"Great," Jenkins said. He fell asleep in seconds.

George returned to his shelter and checked his patient. He hoped the storm passed quickly. The man needed a hospital.

———

The great storm roared through the mountain range. Its wind and snow battered the rock, but the mountains took little notice. They had seen storms far worse than this one for millions of years. And they would see more.

The storm moved past Denali, heading east over the Canadian tundra. It traveled hundreds of miles until it weakened.

Then it was over.

CHAPTER 15

Sergeant George was up and down throughout the night. He kept track of the vital signs of the two men. They were stable, but they needed care. He didn't notice it at first, but the wind had weakened. He poked his head outside the shelter. He saw a cloudless sky.

"Hey, Loot!" George said.

Jenkins groaned and climbed out of his shelter.

"What?" he said.

"Storm's over," Smith said.

"Great. That's great." Jenkins tried the radio. No one answered his calls.

He reached into his ruck for the satellite phone when they both heard it.

A helicopter.

Then sound came over their helmet radios.

"Anybody out there? This is NPS Chopper Seven."

"Jenkins here, is that you Ranger Richmond?" he said.

The chopper flew into view. They gave a thumbs-up as it circled above them.

"It's me," Ranger Richmond said. "We had a scare. Thought we lost you."

"You're not far off," Jenkins said. "It was close."

"I'll bet," Richmond said. "What do you have?"

"Two patients," Jenkins said. "One is Cat Alpha with a possible fractured skull."

"A cat what?" Richmond asked, confused.

"It means he goes first," Jenkins said.

"Roger that," Richmond said. "I'll lower the basket. It's got oxygen, food, and water for you. Load him in, and I'll take him back."

Jenkins and George watched the metal basket slowly descend. They both thought it was a beautiful sight.

"By the way," Richmond said. "I have a message from Sergeant Marks for you."

"Mako!" George said. "He made it?"

"Everyone made it back," Richmond said. "Airman Smith has a dislocated elbow. They all have some bumps and bruises."

"And the climbers?" Jenkins asked.

"Two of the climbers are on the fence with a their toes," said Richmond. "Might lose a few to frostbite. They're hospitalized. Could have been a lot worse. You should be proud of your squad, Lieutenant."

Richmond banked the chopper, circling over them.

"I always am," Jenkins said. "What is the message from Mako?"

Richmond chuckled and said, "He said, and I quote, 'Please quit wasting time and get back to the base camp.'"

"He must be fine, then," said Sergeant George, laughing.

"We all are," Jenkins said. "That's all that matters."

"We did it, Loot," George said.

"Yes, we did, Sergeant. Yes, we did," Jenkins said. He smiled.

Without another word, the two PJs turned to their patients. The job wasn't finished quite yet. Once they were safe, they could relax. Until then, there were things to do so that others may live.

GLOSSARY

CAT ALPHA—short for Category Alpha. A Category Alpha patient is one that is seriously injured and requires immediate medical attention.

COMM CHANNEL—Short for communication channel.

CRAMPONS—Metal plate with spikes fixed to a boot that is used for climbing.

CRO—Combat Rescue Officer. Usually a Lieutenant, the Combat Rescue Officer directs PJs on a mission. Usually from a command post or base.

GOLDEN HOUR—When PJs pull an injured patient off the battlefield, they try to return them to a hospital within one hour. This is called the Golden Hour. Patients who can get medical treatment within the first hour have a better chance of survival.

INDOC—Short for Indoctrination; INDOC is the first stage of PJ training.

JOLLY—the nickname of the Sikorsky MH-53 helicopter; full name is the Jolly Green Giant

LZ—short for Landing Zone

NCO—Non-Commissioned Officer. Termmilitary officers who have not earned a commission

PAST—short for the Physical Ability and Strength Test. Each PJ must pass the test which is made up of various exercises.

PAVE HAWK—she Sikorsky HH-60 Helicopter; used in most PJ missions in combat zones.

PIPELINE—Once a PJ candidate survives INDOC they move to the pipeline. The pipeline includes parachute training, scuba training, and medical training. It takes nearly two years to complete.

PT—Physical training.

RAPPEL—Using a rope to drop from a height, to the ground or a lower level. Often done from helicopters to the ground, if the helicopter is unable to land.

SERE—acronym for Survival Evasion Resistance and Escape. Training that teaches PJs how to escape capture, live off the land, escape and resist interrogation if they are captured or behind enemy lines.

INFORMATION BRIEFING:

DENALI

◎ Location: South-central Alaska

◎ Peak Elevation: 20,310 feet (6,190 meters)

◎ Name History: Officially changed to Denali in 2015 (formerly known as Mount McKinley)

◎ Summiting Denali: Explorer Frederick Cook claimed to have summited Denali in 1906, but this was later disproved. Hudson Stuck, Walter HArper, Harry Karstens, and Robert Tatum first summited Denali in 1913. The youngest person to summit Denali was Galen Johnston, age 11, in 2001.

DENALI THE FIERCE

The weather on Denali is some of the fiercest on the planet. Wind chill temperatures on the mountain have plunged lower than negative-100 degrees. That is cold enough to cause human beings instant death. Because the mountain is so far north, the barometric pressure causes more extreme weather than normal. At over 20,000 feet, and with such extreme weather, Denali has proven to be a difficult mountain to climb. The first climbers scaled the mountain in 1913. The first solo ascent was in 1970.

Most climber rescues on the mountain are conducted by the National Park Service. However, in extreme situations, the Park Service calls on the 212th Pararescue Squadron. The PJ's in the 212th squadron are stationed at Joint Base Elmendorf-Richardson in Anchorage, Alaska.

ABOUT THE AUTHOR

Michael P. Spradlin is the *New York Times* bestselling author of more than thirty books for children and adults. His books include the international bestselling trilogy *The Youngest Templar*, the Edgar nominated *Spy Goddess* series and the Wrangler Award-winning *Off Like the Wind: The First Ride of the Pony Express*. He lives in Lapeer, Michigan. Visit his website at www.michaelspradlin.com.

ABOUT THE ILLUSTRATOR

Spiros Karkavelas is a concept artist and photographer based in Greece. He graduated from Feng Zhu School of Design in Singapore in 2013 and has done work with various video game and book publishing companies. His realistic illustrations often have a theme of modern-day or futuristic warfare, and he draws inspiration from true war stories, the realities of the battlefield, and how war brings out both the worst and best in human nature.

DISCUSSION QUESTIONS

1. Becoming a PJ involves passing numerous physical tests, including running, swimming, survival training, and more. What part of becoming a PJ do you think would be the most difficult? The easiest? Why?

2. The PJ motto is "These Things We Do That Others May Live." Their primary mission is to rescue United States Air Force pilots who have been shot down, often behind enemy lines. What do you think motivates a person to become a PJ and risk their life for others?

3. Research some of the other Special Forces in the United States Military such as the Navy Seals and Delta Force. How do the PJs compare to them? How is their mission the same? How is it different?

WRITING PROMPTS

1. The PJs and most military members use nicknames and acronyms to describe both individuals and objects. Imagine you are the newest member of a PJ unit. Write what your nickname would be and why.

2. Imagine you are a PJ evacuating a patient on the basket hoist to the chopper. In high winds, the hoist jams. How will you rescue the patient? Write the scene.

3. Imagine you are a PJ on a rescue mission to Denali. Your helicopter finds and circles an injured climber, but as you are about to fast rope down, there is a loud boom and . . . avalanche! Write what happens next.

FOLLOW EACH HEROIC MISSION OF
PARARESCUE CORPS

Find cool websites and more books like this
one at **www.facthound.com.**

Just type in the Book ID: 9781496552037
and you're ready to go!